THE HISTORY CHANNEL® PRESENTS

HAUNTED HISTORY™

D0360265

AMERICA'S MOST HAUNTED

BY CAMERON BANKS

SCHOLASTIC INC.
New York   Toronto   London   Auckland   Sydney
Mexico City   New Delhi   Hong Kong   Buenos Aires

No part of this publication may be reproduced in whole or in
part, stored in a retrieval system, or transmitted in any form
or by any means, electronic, mechanical, photocopying,
recording, or otherwise, without written permission of the
publisher. For information regarding permission, write to
Scholastic Inc., Attention: Permissions Department,
557 Broadway, New York, NY 10012.

ISBN 0-439-40150-X

The History Channel, the "H" logo, and HAUNTED
HISTORY are registered trademarks of A&E Television
Networks. All Rights Reserved. © AETN 2002.

Design by Louise Bova

12 11 10 9 8 7 6 5 4 3 2 1   2 3 4 5 6 7/0

Printed in the U.S.A.   40
First Scholastic printing, September 2002

CONTENTS

THE HISTORY CHANNEL® PRESENTS HAUNTED HISTORY™

AMERICA'S MOST HAUNTED

BY CAMERON BANKS

GHOSTS ACROSS AMERICA

They still hang out in Hollywood, roam the Rocky Mountains, and act tough in Tombstone, Arizona. They appear everywhere from New England to New Orleans. Who are they? The ghosts of America's most haunted places, of course!

From the mountains to the prairies, America's spooky specters show history *does* repeat itself in chilling ways! The many people who have actually seen, heard, or even *smelled* ghosts claim it's an experience they'll never forget!

Curious about meeting one of America's "most haunting" yourself? Even if you don't happen to have a ghost, poltergeist, or other spirit in your own neighborhood, you're in luck! This book will take you on a coast-to-coast road trip

HOLLYWOOD

NEW ORLEANS

TOMBSTONE

to find ghosts. You'll travel across the country and through time, hearing from real people who have encountered sights too strange to explain! And you'll meet some of the spookiest historical figures from America's past.

Working with The History Channel, we have tracked down the most awesome apparitions, the strangest specters, and the most ghoulish ghosts. We've found real-life, modern-day witnesses to hauntings. We've gotten to know the ghosts of many places and discovered the stories behind the sightings. And, of course, we want to share these stories with you!

Ready for the eeriest road trip ever? Good! Hop in the hearse, buckle up, and brace yourself for the spookiest sight-seeing around. We're hitting the highway to take a trip through *America's Most Haunted!*

NEW ENGLAND

WILD WEST

ROCKIES

OLD HAUNTS AND WITCH HUNTS

From the shocking Salem witch trials to the amazing Underground Railroad, New England's long, remarkable history has set the stage for some extraordinary apparitions.

SALEM, MASSACHUSETTS:
The Most Haunted Place in America?

Many believe the seaside community of Salem, Massachusetts, has the most horrifying history of any town in America! Founded in 1626 and famous for its witch hunts, Salem's past is spine-chilling!

Witchcraft Mania

When you picture witches, do you think of people dressed up in pointy hats with broom-sticks? Back in the 1600s, ordinary people were accused of being real witches who cast spells to hurt others. And it was a *deadly* serious problem for some Salem residents!

Witch mania first struck the village of Salem in 1692. Two girls, aged nine and eleven, began to suffer from what witnesses called "screaming, convulsive seizures, and trance-like states." A local doctor couldn't explain these strange fits. He declared that someone had put a spell on the girls to harm them. He believed they were victims of witchcraft, a crime at the time.

When the girls accused several Salem residents of casting evil spells, fear and suspicion spread like wildfire through the community. Before long, 141 people were arrested for witchcraft. Their trials became some of the most famous and disturbing in American history.

A woman named Bridget Bishop was the first person in Salem tried as a witch. Found guilty, she was hanged on June 10, 1692. Over the summer, the trials continued. Five men and thirteen women were hanged. Finally, in October, the governor of Massachusetts stopped the witch trials, but the damage was done. That terrible time is said to haunt Salem to this day.

The Corey Curse

A man named Giles Corey was a wealthy Salem landowner. In 1692, Salem Sheriff George Corwin arrested Corey for witchcraft and took him into custody. Sheriff Corwin was known far and wide for his cruelty. Many said he even brought people he arrested to a secret house and tortured them!

THE PHANTOM FILES

Between 1629 and 1642, more than 15,000 men, women, and children sailed from England to the Americas, many settling in New England. While seeking religious freedom in a new land, they brought superstitions from Europe . . . among them, a fear of witches, warlocks, and things that go bump in the night.

In the late 1600s, the government could legally take property from those who confessed to practicing witchcraft. Later, many said Sheriff Corwin misused his authority to steal from people. In the case of Giles Corey, Corwin's cruel tactics to gain a confession were deadly.

An old English law at the time permitted crushing an accused witch under rocks to get them to confess. When Giles Corey refused to speak, Sheriff Corwin ordered the grisly treatment. Even as he lay in agony, Corey would say nothing. But Corey *did* spit out some final words. "I curse you," he told Sheriff Corwin. "And I curse Salem!" Today, Salem residents wonder if the Corey curse still lingers.

PARANORMAL POP QUIZ!

On October 31, 2001, more than three hundred years after they were accused, tried, and hanged as witches on Gallows Hill in Salem, five women were officially exonerated — cleared of all criminal charges — by the state of Massachusetts. True or false?

(answer: true)

Weird Events at the Ward House

Cruel Sheriff Corwin died mysteriously less than five years after Giles Corey was tortured to death at a place called the Joshua Ward House. And for centuries, the house has hosted ghostly activity.

A woman named Julie Tashé bought the historic house in the 1970s to use as offices. She says some activity there is simply strange, like candles melting into weird shapes overnight for no reason! But the house hosts otherworldly events that go beyond weird.

In 1993, when Julie's employees were posing for photographs in the house, a strange image of a young girl appeared in one picture. Was this a ghost, playing a joke on them? Since the spirit enjoyed setting off alarms, removing lamp shades from lamps, and turning over trash baskets, maybe it was!

THE PHANTOM FILES

Did you know that many believe that ghosts are linked to a last thought in a person's life? If they wanted to do something at the moment they were dying, their spirit might attempt to complete that task. A curse like Giles Corey's would be especially powerful — and might continue on longer than a curse uttered at another time.

One evening, a custodian in the Joshua Ward House felt a strange presence. Suddenly, an intense pressure gripped him, pushing him down!

Thinking it was an intruder, he twisted around. But nobody was there!

When another witness visited the house, she saw a very pale elderly lady sitting in the lobby . . . or did she? The witness told us, "She wasn't a live human being, but she was certainly something."

Whatever that "something" is remains a mystery. But it's clear that "something" is also present in the Salem sites linked to Nathaniel Hawthorne, author of *The Scarlet Letter* and one of America's most famous novelists!

UNNATURAL HABITATS: Nathaniel Hawthorne's Haunted Homes

Famous author Nathaniel Hawthorne lived and wrote in Salem in the 1800s. The house where he was born and a house where he later lived called the House of the Seven Gables (the setting for one of his *spookiest* books) are both said to *swarm* with supernatural beings.

Hawthorne's Haunted Birthplace

Nathaniel Hawthorne was born in Salem on July 4, 1804, and many say his first home is among Salem's *hottest* spots for hauntings. What else could explain why objects at the house move around, seemingly by themselves?

House guide Ed Carberg reports that he has found chairs out of place when nobody has moved them. And then there was the clock that's been stopped for years . . . that suddenly started working again. "You'll see a little pendulum going back and forth," he says. The cause? "Probably one of the ghosts," says Carberg.

THE PHANTOM FILES

Did you know that Nathaniel Hawthorne was a direct descendant of Justice John Hathorne, one of the cruel judges at the Salem witch trials? Nathaniel added a "w" to his name, perhaps to distance himself from his notorious ancestor.

The House of the Seven Gables and the Underground Railroad

Susanna Ingersoll was Nathaniel Hawthorne's wealthy cousin who lived in Salem her whole life.

Susanna believed strongly that slavery was wrong. She is said to have offered the House of the Seven Gables as a stop on the Underground Railroad for slaves seeking freedom in the north.

The Underground Railroad was not really underground or a railroad, but 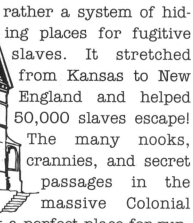 rather a system of hiding places for fugitive slaves. It stretched from Kansas to New England and helped 50,000 slaves escape! The many nooks, crannies, and secret passages in the massive Colonial house would have made it a perfect place for runaway slaves to hide.

Today, many say the spirits of Susanna and some of the runaway slaves live on in the House of the Seven Gables. Tour groups at the huge house have been spooked by a woman said to be Susanna herself! The old-fashioned figure wears a shawl and turban and is seen standing at an upstairs window. And tourists have spotted ghosts of slaves as well. Some experts believe the house holds the energy of people who once hid there, knowing it was a safe place.

LOVE THAT WOULDN'T DIE

A young and handsome couple, Elisha Benton and Jemima Barrows, died during Revolutionary War times. But at the old Daniel Benton Homestead in Tolland, Connecticut, their doomed love may live on forever.

Doomed from the Start?

From the beginning, the relationship between Elisha Benton and Jemima Barrows seemed cursed. The wealthy Benton family didn't want Elisha to marry Jemima, the daughter of a poor cabinetmaker. Despite his family's disapproval, Elisha proposed to Jemima.

PARANORMAL POP QUIZ!

In places where ghost activity is present, visitors often report a feeling of physical heaviness, almost as if something is weighing down on them.
True or false?

(answer: true)

In 1775, Elisha was called to fight in the War of Independence. Before he left Tolland, Elisha vowed to come back to Jemima someday. And he promised they would marry when he returned.

The Promise of a Prisoner

In 1776, Elisha was captured during a battle and became a prisoner on a ship harbored in the Long Island Sound. With no sanitation and little food, the prison ships were a breeding ground for smallpox, a serious and contagious disease. Someone who caught smallpox could die from it — there was no cure at the time.

Elisha was stricken with smallpox. But as the war came to a close, he kept his promise to Jemima and returned to Tolland.

THE PHANTOM FILES

There are many theories about why ghosts visit some places again and again. Some claim ghosts return to troubled places. But others say that ghosts return to places where they felt more at peace than anywhere else on Earth, such as a favorite room or a quiet spot.

'Til Death Do Us Part . . .

As soon as she heard Elisha had returned, Jemima rushed to the Benton home to see him. But smallpox can spread quickly. Jemima was not allowed inside.

Jemima *had* to see Elisha. She asked the

Bentons if she could care for him herself, sparing the family from more exposure to smallpox. At the same time, she knew she was putting herself in danger.

Sealed off from the rest of the house, with food and water left by the door, Jemima did what she could for Elisha. But on January 21, 1777, he died. About a month later, on February 28, Jemima died as well. Today, the spirit of Jemima may live on in the house, still searching for Elisha, her one true love.

Ghostly Appearances

When two students spent a night in the Benton Homestead, they heard strange voices floating up from the basement, but when they investigated, nobody was there! And when they opened a door to an upstairs room, they felt a bone-shivering chill.

At 4:00 A.M., one of the students felt a strong urge to look through the doorway to the room where Elisha Benton had passed away. But she also felt terrified, she says. Finally, she looked up. "I forced myself to do it. And as I did, something had been there looking at me. . . . Unfortunately, it disappeared." Was it the spirit of Elisha or Jemima? It's still a mystery.

A couple who once rented the homestead reports strange events as well. The woman says she woke up to see a man standing by the edge of her bed. Half asleep, she thought it was her husband. But when she felt a hand clamp over her mouth, she knew it was something sinister. When she pushed the hand away, it evaporated into thin air! Finally awake, she saw her husband sleeping soundly beside her. To this day, she still doesn't know exactly who or what was there that night — or *why*. There is still no way to explain it!

The same might be said for the amazing apparitions and events in so many of New England's historic houses. With some of the oldest and richest history in the nation, New England's haunting tradition goes way back — and will probably continue for a long, long time.

New Orleans, Louisiana

VOODOO QUEENS AND A HAUNTED *DELTA QUEEN*

Nicknamed "the Big Easy" and the "Crescent City," New Orleans, Louisiana, has a long, spirited tradition. With a fascinating history featuring everything from voodoo queens to hauntings on a riverboat called the *Delta Queen*, New Orleans is home to some of the most bizarre apparitions anywhere.

THE VOODOO QUEEN

Voodoo began in New Orleans in the early 1800s as a religion that is an unusual mix of traditional African beliefs and Roman Catholicism. One of the most famous early spiritual leaders of voodoo is voodoo queen Marie Laveau, whose spirit is still sometimes spotted in New Orleans.

VOODOO Power

Born in 1794, Marie Laveau was a "free

woman of color" whose ancestors included people who were black, white, and Native American. While supporting herself as a hairdresser for wealthy white and Creole women, Marie learned the practices of voodoo. Her reputation grew, and people of all colors came to her for aid and advice.

Soon, Marie Laveau became the most famous voodoo "queen" in all of New Orleans. Under her guidance, the yearly voodoo rituals on St. John's Eve (June 23rd) at Lake Pontchartrain became huge, spectacular events.

Marie Laveau became best known for her voodoo help on behalf of an aristocratic young man who was accused of a violent crime and awaiting trial. The voodoo queen first mixed up a special *gris-gris* —a combination of herbs, roots, and oils — and put it in a bag. She left the bag on the judge's doorstep with a note stating the young man's innocence. In the final part of her ritual,

THE PHANTOM FILES

Did you know that voodoo, or voudon, began to evolve because practicing African beliefs was forbidden in America? "Voodooists" saw similarities between African gods and Catholic saints. Voodoo evolved into a combination of the two religions that is still practiced today.

Marie put three peppers in her mouth, then placed them under the judge's chair. And what was the judge's final verdict? Not guilty!

Long "Live" the Queen!

For followers of voodoo, Marie Laveau's spirit lives on in New Orleans parlors where practitioners still mix *gris-gris* potions. But even to nonbelievers, the spirit of the voodoo queen may still be present in New Orleans.

Some say the ghost of Marie Laveau haunts Saint Louis Cemetery Number One, where she is buried. More than a century after her death, Laveau's gravesite is still one of the most commonly visited. The front of the tomb is marked by a series of red X's that visitors make as a form of voodoo prayer. Sightings of the voodoo queen are common there, some say!

PARANORMAL POP QUIZ!

To thank voodoo queen Marie Laveau for her help, the young aristocrat's grateful family gave her *Maison Blanche,* or "White House," which became the site of much voodoo activity in New Orleans. True or false?

(answer: true)

Still others believe that the kind spirit of Marie Laveau has taken the shape of a crow that flies through the city. Many feel that this helpful, magical woman is still keeping watch over her beloved city.

A TRUE HOUSE OF HORRORS

The house on Royal Street in New Orleans' French Quarter may *look* ordinary, but its horrifying history is anything but! Once the site of a true-life torture chamber, the scary spirits of earlier inhabitants may still hang around the mansion.

Hidden Evil

In the 1830s, the LaLauries were a rich, well-regarded couple. They were members of New Orleans high society. Madame Delphine Macarty LaLaurie was a Southern belle known throughout the city for her lavish entertaining. Her husband was a highly respected physician. They appeared to be the perfect couple at the grand balls they threw at their Royal Street mansion. But what actually went on in the LaLauries' house was perfectly *evil*.

When a fire broke out at the LaLaurie mansion on April 10, 1834, firefighters discovered a strange, barred door leading to the attic. They forced the door open and found a horrifying, grisly scene. The mutilated bodies of seven slaves, thought to be victims of the LaLauries' torture, hung there!

THE PHANTOM FILES

The rich history of New Orleans reflects the influences of French and Spanish settlers and African slaves. A unique blend of various cultures, the city is the proud birthplace of American jazz music, which combined European and African influences. Louis Armstrong, Fats Waller, and many other jazz musicians became famous throughout the world for introducing a whole new sound.

Word of the atrocities spread fast. Outraged citizens tried to track down the brutal LaLauries and bring them to justice. Although the couple fled

New Orleans, many say that spirits of the evil LaLauries and their innocent victims may remain in the house on Royal Street.

Skeletons and Spooky Sightings

In the late 1800s, workers renovating the LaLaurie house made another staggering discovery. Beneath the floorboards, they found several human skeletons! Even weirder, many of the mansion's owners and their employees have reported frightening incidents involving the spirit of the infamous LaLauries and their victims.

A servant in the house claimed that he awoke one night to find himself being choked by none other than Madame LaLaurie! He described his attacker as a pale woman with dark hair and a crazed look in her eyes. Another pair of dark hands broke her grip on his throat, he said, and the ghost screamed and disappeared!

The house hosts other spirits of slaves. Unlike the ghost of their evil mistress, the slaves in the

LaLaurie house have never done any harm. In the 1890s, the mansion became a boardinghouse. A tenant sighted a man who was bound in chains sitting on the staircase. When he approached the strange figure, it disappeared!

PLANTATION PHANTASMS

As New Orleans grew, so did the plantations surrounding the city. In 1796, General David Bradford built the Myrtles Plantation on land that was once used by the Tunica Indians as a burial ground. It would become one of the most infamous haunted sites in the South.

Cruel and Unusual Punishment

General Bradford's daughter, Sara Matilda, married Judge Clark Woodruff, who began to run the plantation. Soon, the couple had three daughters named Mary, Jane, and Octavia. The family had many servants, including a girl named Chloe, who took care of the children.

Chloe was a slave. Her job in the Myrtles plantation house made it possible for her to hear information that might affect her and other slaves, and she shared news with others about upcoming sales or trades that might break up families. All went well until the day Chloe was caught eavesdropping. As punishment, one of her ears was cut off!

Chloe's Revenge

From that day on, Chloe wore a scarf to cover her wound. But one day, when Judge Woodruff was away on business, she came up with a plan for revenge.

Secretly, Chloe boiled the leaves of an oleander plant. The oleander plant creates a strong poison when its leaves are boiled. Chloe added the poison to the batter of a birthday cake for one of the chil-

THE PHANTOM FILES

Native American burial grounds are common locations for supernatural activity. Ghosts are often found in places where sacred burial land has been taken over and used for other purposes.

dren. Although nobody knows for sure what Chloe *really* meant to do, some historians believe she just wanted to make the family sick, so she could come to their rescue! But disaster struck. While baby Octavia slept safely, Jane, Mary, and their mother, Sara Matilda, ate the cake . . . and died!

After Chloe confessed to the poisoning, she was hanged by an angry mob of black and white people on the plantation grounds. While that was the last time anyone ever saw Chloe, the same isn't said of her victims.

Ghostly Playmates

The Myrtles is now a bed-and-breakfast, but many say it's still home for some ghostly little girls and their mother! One night, a guest arrived late in the evening and saw a young girl dressed in a white gown, sitting on a bed. The guest thought the child was the daughter of friends staying at The Myrtles, and the next morning, commented to them about how much the child had grown. Yet there was one shocking detail: The friends hadn't brought their daughter on the trip!

PARANORMAL POP QUIZ!

In the 1790s, General David Bradford paid $5.00 an acre for the land outside of New Orleans where he built his plantation. True or false?

(answer: false)
He only paid $1.25 an acre!

Who *was* that girl on the bed? Nobody knows for sure, but others have reported sightings of the murdered girls. Children staying at the bed-and-breakfast say they've played with some strange little girls on the grounds — when no other children were guests there! Others say they've seen a pale woman standing on the main staircase and have heard strange footsteps on the back stairs — when nobody is there!

THE PHANTOM FILES

The Myrtles hosts other ghosts as well. In fact, some say it is the most haunted location in America, with *fourteen* known specters in residence!

THE HAUNTED RIVERBOAT

From 1811 to 1900, steamboats powered development and trade all along the Mississippi River. One such ship, the *Delta Queen*, has a fascinating ghostly past *and* present.

Apparitions Aboard!

When steamboats were first introduced in the early 1800s, they revolutionized trade and travel.

A hundred years later, the faster, more reliable railroad put many steamboat lines out of business. But Captain Gordon C. Greene of New Orleans still believed in paddle-wheel riverboats and started a company called the Delta Queen Steamboat Company.

By 1895, Greene's wife, Mary, had also become a full-fledged riverboat captain. When Captain Greene died in 1927, Mary and her sons took over the riverboat business. By the 1940s, Mary and her son Captain

THE PHANTOM FILES

The *Delta Queen* isn't the only haunted ship around. Many sea vessels, including the ocean liner the *Queen Mary,* are also famous for ghost sightings!

Tom purchased a boat they christened the *Delta Queen*, and after a renovation that included fitting out a room aboard the ship as Mary's home, the steamboat made its maiden voyage on June 30, 1948. Mary piloted the vessel herself in its early months. Captain Mary died in 1949. She had been a riverboat captain for fifty-five years. But it's said that her spirit still inhabits the famous ship!

Encounters with Captain Mary

There was something close to his ear. And it felt like breath blowing. That's how First Mate Mike Williams described why he rose from his bunk one night in 1982. He was alone on the *Delta Queen*. Thinking someone had come on board, he began searching the ship. A door slammed loudly, startling him. But nothing was there. He walked toward the engine room. A large pipe was leaking, and water was gushing everywhere!

Mike says that if he hadn't woken up, the *Delta Queen* might have filled with water and sunk! He believes that "there's a benevolent, gentle, old lady who keeps an eye out over the boat. I'm sure it's Captain Mary Greene."

Though Mike Williams never saw Mary B. Greene himself, others aboard the *Delta Queen* have. The ship's historian, Marcie Richardson, says she has seen Mary reading in one of the vessel's lounges late at night. But when the witness did a double take, the female sea captain vanished!

Late one evening, ship entertainer Phyllis Dale encountered a lady in a long green velvet robe who also disappeared without explanation! But these sort of sightings aren't too unusual on the *Delta Queen*. In fact, as long as the ship sails, Captain Mary B. Greene will probably be there, looking out for her passengers.

From haunted riverboats to voodoo parlors, few places have the assortment of ghosts documented in the Crescent City. It seems the spirits of New Orleans are as diverse, exciting, and colorful as the town itself!

Tombstone, Arizona

THE "TOWN TOO TOUGH TO DIE"

Welcome to the Wild, Wild West! With a notorious history of outlaws, gunfighters, and just plain colorful characters, Tombstone, Arizona, *defined* "Wild West" in the 1880s. Tombstone's heyday was short, but its infamous inhabitants still roam the streets.

TOMBSTONE'S HISTORY AT A GLANCE

In 1877, a man named Ed Schieffelin went looking for silver mines in the land about seventy miles southeast of Tucson, Arizona. Many said the only thing he would find on that barren Apache land would be his tombstone. But in the nearby Dragoon Mountains, he found silver, and lots of it! Schieffelin struck it rich and put the town of Tombstone on the map.

Word of the mining town with the

strange and spooky name spread, and the town grew very quickly. Tombstone's rough-and-tumble reputation grew as well. In the early 1880s, it had more gambling houses, dance halls, and saloons than any other town in the Southwest!

Tombstone's "silver rush" didn't last long, however. Within a decade, the mines flooded, and this slowed its rapid growth. By the early 1900s, the price of silver dropped, and Tombstone seemed doomed. Although the Great Depression of the 1930s, floods, and fires threatened Tombstone over the years, it still survives as a vibrant tourist town today. Many call it the "town too tough to die." Those who have met the spirits of Tombstone swear the town's *toughest* still thrive there!

THE PHANTOM FILES

Just how fast did Tombstone grow? In 1879, it had forty cabins and a hundred people. By 1880, 3,000 people lived there; by late 1881, Tombstone's population grew to more than 7,000 people. A year later, there were more than 10,000 people in the town! However, not long after, it would nearly become a *ghost town.*

SHOWDOWN AT THE O.K. CORRAL

No history of Tombstone would be complete without the story of the legendary shootout between federal marshalls and cattle rustlers at the O.K. Corral. And no haunted history would be complete without mentioning the outlaws who *still* stalk the place!

Have you ever seen a door unlock itself, or lights that turn on with no cause? These strange sights are common at the O.K. Corral, some say. But no sight is more amazing than the O.K. Corral's full apparition of a mur-dered gun-slinger!

Billy Clanton Returns

On October 26, 1881, famous lawmen Wyatt Earp, Virgil Earp, and Doc Holliday ambushed outlaws from the McLowery-Clanton gang at the O.K.

THE PHANTOM FILES

Did you know that Tombstone mines are located under the town itself? Several mines, such as the Vizinia, the Mountain Maid, and the Gilded Age even open up right in the middle of several buildings in town!

Corral. Three gang members died, including huge, eighteen-year-old Billy Clanton. Known as one of the nastiest members of the gang, Billy is still seen wandering the O.K. Corral, perhaps seeking revenge.

The mysterious cowboy appears in old-fashioned western gear, prowling around the O.K. Corral. Says one witness, "I heard footsteps coming across the dirt. I saw a gentleman . . . in 1880s clothing." And how did it feel to see a real ghost? The witness says the experience was actually hair-raising! But, she says, "It was really awesome to know they are real. And they're here."

THE PHANTOM FILES

Strange, unexplained appearances of light are signs of paranormal activity. These apparitions take many different forms, including round orbs.

Virgil Earp Returns, Too!

Outlaws aren't the only ones returning from the dead in Tombstone! Virgil Earp was once Tombstone's deputy and the brother of famed marshall Wyatt Earp. Two months after the gunfight at the O.K. Corral, Virgil was shot in the back *nineteen times* by three unknown assassins outside of Tombstone's Crystal Palace Bar.

About fifty people a year claim to see Earp's ghost at the same spot in Tombstone. He's a mysterious man dressed in a black frock coat and wide-brimmed hat. Sometimes he walks toward people. And sometimes, he simply stares at them. Maybe the legendary lawman is still keeping the peace in his town.

BUMPS IN THE NIGHT AT BUFORD HOUSE

Built in 1880, the Buford House is now a bed-and-breakfast. But it was once the site of tragedy, which may explain why it's a magnet for haunting activity today.

The tragedy began in the 1880s, when Buford House resident George Dawes fell in love with a girl named Patra Edmonds, who lived across the street.

PARANORMAL POP QUIZ!

Tombstone's Allen Street was once home to 106 bars and much violent activity. A man who once kept a wolf as a pet in Tombstone couldn't go down the street with the creature because the animal was spooked by the supernatural activity there. True or false?

(answer: true)

Patra was known to always wear a certain perfume that smelled of lavender. To earn money for their wedding, George worked in a mine forty miles away. When he returned to Tombstone nine months later, he saw Patra take the arm of another man. Crazed with jealousy, he grabbed a gun and shot Patra four times! Convinced he had killed her, he then shot himself and died.

But Patra didn't die! A doctor removed the bullets and saved her life. Today, though, many visitors to Buford House detect a scent of lavender that comes from nowhere. Could this smell be linked to Patra's past?

George's body is gone, but Tombstone legend says his spirit lives on in the Buford House. The current owners of the Buford House say they even encountered George at Christmas in 1999! They reported that a creepy, shadowy figure of a young man in western clothes kept peering in at their family, watching as they put up their Christmas tree!

"BOO"S IN THE BIRD CAGE

Tombstone's Bird Cage Theater opened on Christmas Day 1881. It soon became known as the most notorious gambling hall in America! At night, some say you can still hear sounds that once filled the Bird Cage. Listen closely, and you might hear music and laughter, the clanking of gold, the clicking of dice, and the sounds of lost souls from the 1880s.

Famous for at least sixteen shootings, the Bird Cage still has more than one hundred bullet holes in its ceiling. And they're not the *only* reminder of the saloon's incredible past.

THE PHANTOM FILES

In the 1880s, Tombstone's Bird Cage Theater was so infamous that even the *New York Times* wrote about it! Open twenty-four hours a day, it offered the finest French champagne, glittering entertainment, and big-money gambling to high rollers from all over.

Spiteful Spirits at a Séance

Employees say the saloon still fills with cigar

smoke and the smell of cheap lilac perfume! The perfume may be a reminder of a fearsome female killer named Gold Dollar, who cut the heart out of a beautiful young woman named Margarita in a jealous rage one evening! Many believe that the angry spirit of Margarita may explain the unseen "something" that nearly choked a man to death at a séance not long ago.

When a medium tried to contact spirits at the Bird Cage, something grabbed Bird Cage owner Bill Hunley around the neck! Hunley began squeezing his wife's hand so hard that she screamed. "They [the other people at the séance] realized my face was turning blue and I was being choked," he recalls. It was the only time Hunley had ever met an

THE PHANTOM FILES

Some people believe that a séance is a way to communicate with departed spirits. The person who is said to be able to contact and even attract spirits is called a "medium." During a séance, a medium might go into a trance, and the spirit is said to speak "through" that person. Once contacted, the ghost may even join the group!

unfriendly spirit at the Bird Cage. But it was an experience he'd *never* want to repeat!

THE SPECTERS OF THE SAN JOSÉ HOUSE

The San José Boarding House in Tombstone has been a hostel — a place to stay — for weary travelers for a long time. And it's also a spot for wayward ghosts! Come along and meet some of these superspooky guests.

Doc Holliday on holiday?

During the years when the West was most *wild*, some of the scariest characters around lived in Tombstone. Doc Holliday was a local lawman and one of the town's most famous citizens. Doc Holliday was a frequent visitor at the San José House in the 1880s and always stayed in one particular room.

PARANORMAL POP QUIZ!

The ghosts at Tombstone's Aztec House seem to bother *only* men, never women! True or false?

(answer: false. The Aztec House was once a boardinghouse for men, and its ghosts seem to want to frighten only women now!)

In fact, some say Doc Holliday liked staying in that room so much that he *never left*.

A guest who requested Doc Holliday's room reported several strange occurrences. The door to the room kept opening and shutting, so the guest locked it. But somehow, the door unlocked again —and it began opening and closing! Next, the guest heard noises coming from the bathroom, as

THE PHANTOM FILES

The apparition of a woman thief who was hung in Tombstone more than a century ago has been seen wandering the town streets for the last *ninety years!*

if someone was flushing the toilet. He checked, but no one was there! It's no surprise that the guest wasn't able to sleep a wink that night.

The next day, the guest decided to take some pictures of the room with a Polaroid camera. His secretary posed in different places in the room but she kept appearing as a haze in the pictures! Thinking something was

wrong with the film or camera, the guest asked his secretary to photograph him. According to Kelly McKechnie, owner of the San José House, the guest himself came out clear as a bell!

Did old Doc dislike having a woman in his room and *float in* to mess up the photo? Perhaps!

THE HISTORY CHANNEL. Some experts say that ghosts rarely linger in graveyards, as they have no real connection to the place. But this photo proves that may not be the case. . . .

Ghosts will sometimes show up in photos as vague, light-filled figures. Could this be a photograph that contains paranormal activity? Or is this simply a result of overexposure by a broken camera? You decide!

This is the riverboat *Delta Queen*, one of New Orleans' most famous ships, as it steams across the Mississippi River. A guest on this beautiful old riverboat would be surprised to learn that it's still haunted by its former captain Mary B. Greene!

This is voodoo queen Marie Laveau's tombstone in the St. Louis Cemetery Number One in New Orleans. Many of Marie's followers have made red X's on the tombstone and left flowers. The celebrated voodoo queen is still a strong presence in the Crescent City, and some say her spirit will never leave!

THE HISTORY CHANNEL®

Many in the town of Tombstone, Arizona, believe that the spirits of long-dead cowboys and gunslingers still roam the Wild West . . . and most of them aren't too friendly.

The famous magician Harry Houdini was fascinated by ghosts and hauntings, as this poster advertising one of his stunts proves. His wife, Bess, often tried to contact him in a séance . . . but did she ever succeed?

THE HISTORY CHANNEL.

This is a picture of old Hollywood and the original Hollywoodland sign. The glamorous celebrities who lived in old-time Hollywood often come back to visit the modern-day town . . . as ghosts!

Good night, ghost

The spirit of Doc Holliday may simply enjoy playing tricks on unsuspecting guests. But some ghosts at the San José House are anything but friendly. Kelly McKechnie reports a personal paranormal experience that she was sure would lead to her death! Imagine encountering a spirit who seems to want to crush you. . . .

It happened one night after Kelly had gone to bed. She reports that she felt her bed sink down, "like someone's knee was in the mattress." Before she knew it, she says she felt a heavy weight on her. "It was so heavy I could hardly breathe." Struggling to free herself, Kelly began to pray for the evil spirit — *or whatever it was* — to go away!

Finally, the mysterious and horrifying pressure stopped. Kelly sat straight up in bed, sweating and shaken. She saw that the chain and dead bolt still locked the bedroom door, and the room was empty! Still, she was terrified, convinced that a dark part of Tombstone's past had come back to haunt her. . . .

From tantalizing tales of treachery and jealousy to the action-packed legends of lawmen, Tombstone's notorious past captures the "spirit" of the American West. And for the many who have met the ghosts of Tombstone, there's no doubt that the town really is "too tough to die"!

The Rocky Mountains

GHOST TOWNS AND CITY SPECTERS

For centuries, the mist-shrouded slopes and granite peaks of Colorado's Rocky Mountains have lured those seeking adventure. And their ghosts still linger in the mysterious mountain area.

HANGIN' OUT WITH SPIRITS IN BUCKSKIN JOE

A thriving mining town in the 1860s, Buckskin Joe fell on hard times and became a ghost town. About a century later, it was moved ninety miles away and rebuilt as a tourist attraction. In this town made up of authentic old buildings, each with its own dramatic history, Buckskin Joe employees report many ghost sightings and creepy events.

The Man in the Mirror

It's said the "Creepiest History" award for a

building at Buckskin Joe goes to a barn once used for public hangings! In the winter months, the building also stored bodies for burial after the spring thaw. Today, the large barn houses a restaurant, a theater, two saloons, an ice cream parlor, and several ghosts!

Staff members say a dark-haired gunfighter appears regularly at the building. The mystery man wears black pants, shirt, and cowboy boots, and has been spotted by both adults and children. After closing the ice cream parlor late one afternoon, an employee was washing dishes. She looked in the mirror and saw the man walk in. But when she turned around, nobody was there!

THE PHANTOM FILES

The town of Buckskin Joe originally got its name from a scruffy-looking old prospector named Joseph Higgenbottom who always wore buckskins. An old story says that he sold his claim to a gold mine for some food and a pistol . . . while others made millions from the mine! He never made money, but Buckskin Joe's name lives on.

So the employee turned back to begin washing dishes again. Glancing into the mirror, she saw the gunfighter once more! What happened next is too eerie to explain easily. "I asked him to leave, and I watched him walk out of the room through the mirror!" she says.

More Spirits Hanging Around

Not all of the spirits at the old hanging barn at Buckskin Joe are so easygoing, however. People who died there either committed a terrible crime or were falsely accused of one. A clairvoyant reader and healer says the grisly history of the place makes it a magnet for paranormal activity. "These beings may or may not be fully leaving the earth realm when they leave their bodies," she says. In other words, there may be many tortured souls in the barn who want to right old wrongs or seek revenge.

A mean-looking old miner that an employee saw in the barn early one morning is just one spirit who refuses to leave! General Manager Vicky Casey says the employee "got a really evil feeling" from the scowling old spirit. Looking up again, he saw the miner a second time. Gripped with fear, the employee felt the hairs on the back of his neck stand up. Realizing that the miner wasn't going anywhere, the employee left the building fast and didn't look back!

MANITOU SPRINGS: SPIRITS' FACES AND COFFIN RACES

In the late nineteenth century, Colorado's Manitou Springs had become a health resort for wealthy Easterners suffering from tuberculosis. A young Bostonian named Emma Crawford was one of these visitors who is still seen there.

Making regular stays at Manitou Springs with her mother, Emma Crawford soon became a beloved member of the community. An excellent pianist, the kind, dark-haired young woman gave concerts and lessons.

THE PHANTOM FILES

Long before European settlers came to the Rockies, the Ute Indians believed the natural springs at Manitou had powerful healing properties. Water from the springs contained minerals thought to heal both the body and spirit. By the 1880s, the Ute were gone. But stories of the mineral springs' cure had spread, and Manitou Springs became a popular resort town.

And although Emma suffered from tuberculosis and exercise was probably difficult for her, she often took walks in the mountains.

Emma liked Red Mountain best, and even renamed it Red Chief Mountain in honor of the Native Americans who once lived there. Wearing a long red dress, the pale young woman would climb the heights of the craggy hills to contact their spirits. And Emma Crawford may still wander that rocky mountaintop to this day.

THE PHANTOM FILES

The deadly lung disease tuberculosis was very common in the 1880s. Fresh air, sunshine, and pure water were thought to help people heal from the disease. Many people left dark, crowded, and polluted cities in the East and headed to the undeveloped mountains of the West to recover.

High in the Sunshine and Pure Air

By 1891, Emma had fallen in love with Wilhelm Hildenbrand, an engineer who came to Manitou to help construct a railroad. The couple would often climb Red Mountain to plan their future. On one visit, Emma asked Hildenbrand to

bury her on that mountaintop, should she die before him. Afraid of cemeteries, she said she wanted a grave high in the sunshine and pure air.

In December, Emma died suddenly, and Wilhelm honored her final wish. It took twenty-four men to carry the coffin up the slippery granite hillside, but Emma was buried on top of Red Mountain! Within a decade, however, developers had decided to build in her final resting place. They dug up the grave and moved Emma's coffin to the other side of the mountain.

Over the years, snow, rain, and spring thaws washed away the earth, and the coffin disintegrated! Local boys even found pieces of the casket that had slid down the mountain! Finally, authorities gathered Emma's bones and reburied her in town. But those who climb Red Mountain today say Emma is still there to greet them! A dark-haired, pale young woman in an old-fashioned red dress has been seen wandering the mountains.

THE PHANTOM FILES

Did you know that one in ten people surveyed say that they have seen or been in the presence of a ghost?

Go, Coffin, Go!

Red Mountain isn't the only place in Manitou Springs where the spirit of Emma Crawford appears. Down in town, the people who recently restored her old house say her spirit still plays beautiful melodies on the piano. And the ghost of Emma has been sighted in windows and standing in doorways!

The people of Manitou cherish the memory of Emma. They think of her as a gentle, kindly spirit who watches over them from on high. To celebrate her spirit, the town holds an annual *coffin* race! Each year, ghoulish costumed competitors race through the streets of Manitou Springs . . . and the fastest casket wins!

THE "UNSINKABLE" BROWN HOUSE

You may have heard of brave Molly Brown, who was best known for being "unsinkable" on the doomed ship *Titanic*. If you've ever seen movies about the incredible shipwreck, you know that she courageously led others in her lifeboat to safety. What is equally amazing is that her grand, historic Denver home may continue to house spirits that just won't *die*!

The Browns: Still in Town?

Built in the late 1800s, the Brown mansion in Denver is now a museum. But it was once the home of millionaire J.J. Brown and his lively wife, Molly. Country boy J.J. had struck it rich in gold mining, and Molly insisted they move to

Denver. Though Molly loved giving big society parties, J.J. longed for a simpler life. Eventually, they separated, and each died. But Brown family members and their staff are said to still reside in the house!

During his life, J.J. was known for slipping away during Molly's parties to go have a smoke by himself. Today, despite a strict no-smoking policy in the museum, people swear there's often the unexplained smell of fresh cigar smoke! Many say they've also seen a grumpy-looking butler who walks down the mansion stairs — then disappears!

Museum employees report seeing a female spirit dressed in Victorian clothing. She wanders the hallway upstairs and often joins groups of visitors! Some speculate the spirit is Molly Brown herself. Others say it's Molly's mother. Regardless of her identity, staff members agree that this friendly spirit still has great affection for the grand, historic home!

THE STANLEY HOTEL: Where They Don't Check Out

In Estes Park, Colorado, the colossal Stanley Hotel sits high on a hill overlooking town. Built in 1909, the hotel even inspired horror master Stephen King, who wrote part of his ghostly novel *The Shining* while staying there.

The Earl and the Inventor

Many say that the Stanley Hotel is still the home to both the American inventor who built the place and the European earl who once owned the land there and lost it. One of the spirits may simply be staying in the home he loved.

PARANORMAL POP QUIZ!

In 1897, F.O. Stanley and his twin brother, Francis, developed a steam-powered automobile called the "Stanley Steamer." The Stanley "Tea Kettle" racer set a land speed record of 127.9 m.p.h. in 1906.
True or false?

(answer: true)

But the other may be hanging around the hotel, looking for revenge.

Long ago, an Irish earl named Lord Dunraven laid a homesteader's claim to several thousand acres in the beautiful Estes Park area. But when others argued a foreigner's homestead claim was not legal, he lost the land. Inventor F.O. Stanley then bought the land, built the luxury hotel, and managed it with his wife until their deaths in the 1940s.

And they may still be there! A hotel desk manager says he "felt that there was someone watching me" and spotted the ghost of Stanley himself. Bellmen have seen the ghost of Mrs. Stanley descend the grand staircase, and guests have complained of hearing her play the piano! Lord Dunraven also has been seen in the hotel. Reports of his smoking in no-smoking areas, hurling eyeglasses, and throwing a wedding ring down the drain show he may still feel the land and hotel should be his!

Fourth-floor Phantoms

For many years, the Stanley Hotel's fourth floor housed servants of wealthy guests. Today, few places *anywhere* have the apparition activity of that area! From unexplained music playing to poltergeists that move guests' belongings, tales of incredible events abound there.

Room 418 was the site of an especially amazing occurrence. One day, the hotel's executive housekeeper inspected the room. It looked great, so he locked the door and walked away. But as he headed down the hallway, the door opened! He went back, locked it, walked away . . . and the door opened again. Thinking someone inside was playing a prank on him, he walked into the room. Nobody was there.

It's said that the restless spirit of a long-dead servant may still haunt the hotel room. Like others willing to risk everything to move to the majestic Rocky Mountains, perhaps the spirit sought adventure. Maybe she was seeking physical or spiritual health. Or perhaps, like so many ghosts of the Rocky Mountains, she is still searching for *something*. . . .

⑤ Hollywood, California

HAUNTED HOTELS AND SPOOKY MOVIE STUDIOS

In just one hundred years, the tiny colony that sprang up on the outskirts of Los Angeles has become the movie-making capital of the world. From haunted hotels to spooky movie studios, Hollywood's history features some of the most famous ghosts anywhere!

SPOOKY CELEBRITY SIGHTINGS!

When you hear the words *movie star*, who springs to mind? Will Smith, Sarah Michelle Gellar, Haley Joel Osment, and Drew Barrymore are some of Hollywood's hottest. Since the 1920s, Hollywood has been home to big-screen stars. And like the celebs of today, these stars led exciting and glamorous lives.

The old stars' glamour lives on at three of Tinseltown's most elegant hotels, where you might just glimpse a celebrity . . . or the ghost of one!

Celebrity Reruns?

At the Roosevelt Hotel on Hollywood Boulevard, guests report seeing well-dressed ghosts in the hallways, walking through walls, and even playing the piano!

Built in 1927 by silent-screen stars Mary Pickford and Douglas Fairbanks, Sr., the Roosevelt was the first luxury hotel in Hollywood. Just like Hollywood hot spots today, the hotel attracted movie stars from the start. Old-time screen legends such as Clark Gable, Carole Lombard, and Marilyn Monroe were just a few of the hotel's famous guests.

THE PHANTOM FILES

Did you know that Hollywood's name comes from a flimsy sign that real estate developers placed high in the hills on the edge of Los Angeles? At first, the sign read HOLLYWOODLAND, but the last four letters of the sign fell down, leaving the name *Hollywood*. What caused the letters to drop is a mystery, but the neighborhood's name stuck! Today, Hollywood and its white-lettered sign are famous the world over.

Marilyn in the Mirror

Imagine seeing Natalie Portman, Jennifer Love Hewitt, or Cameron Diaz in person. It could happen in Hollywood!

And, say some Hollywood insiders, you might just see some old-time stars still hanging around the Roosevelt! As a young model, movie star Marilyn Monroe got her first break in Hollywood posing by the hotel's pool. Later, the blond beauty often stayed at the hotel. Marilyn died in 1962, but some say the image of Monroe still appears in a mirror that once hung in the screen legend's favorite suite!

The Haunted Blossom Ballroom

It's always exciting to watch the Oscars on television and try to guess who's going to win. In 1929, the first Oscar *ever* was awarded at the first Academy Awards banquet, which took place at the Roosevelt Hotel's Blossom Ballroom. In the years following that special event, the ballroom has hosted other happenings that are more strange than special.

Many report a mysterious "cold spot" in the Blossom Ballroom. Witnesses describe the small area as very chilly, even when the rest of the room is warm. And when you stand by the "cold spot," you feel an odd surge of energy that's impossible to explain!

Perhaps most startling is the ballroom's bizarre "man in black" who appears out of nowhere! The hotel's catering manager says a mysterious, ghostly man clad entirely in black shows up in the "cold spot" in the center of the ballroom. Witnesses say they feel his spine-chilling presence before he appears.

PARANORMAL POP QUIZ!

Some parapsychologists believe that "cold spots" indicate a place like a portal, where spirits transport in and out of the earthly world.
True or false?

(answer: true)

The Haunted Landmark

For more than seventy-five years, the land-mark Hollywood Knickerbocker Hotel has been a gathering place for big-name celebrities. Elvis Presley, Frank Sinatra, and even the Three Stooges were once guests there! And now, many say the Knickerbocker is a center of supernatural activity.

A strange lady ghost walks through the hotel's walls, some report. In the café, lights flick on and off with no explanation, cups rattle on their own in the sink, and books move unassisted! Even back in the 1920s and 1930s, séances were held in the hotel by Bess Houdini, who may have contacted her dead husband, the famous magician Harry Houdini!

THE PHANTOM FILES

To determine whether ghosts are present, parapsychologists use a tool called a magnetometer that measures electromagnetic energy fields. A ghost, specter, poltergeist, or other entity can actually generate an electromagnetic field the device measures.

While he was still alive, Houdini often promised his wife he would try to contact her from beyond if he died. Did he succeed? No one knows for sure. Reports of a weird white mist and sightings of ghostly celebrities in the nearby rest rooms are common. And according to a well-known parapsychologist, two investigators of the hotel's rest rooms identified a ghostly woman from the 1940s who was joined by another female apparition. Without a doubt, the parapsychologist says, "The Knickerbocker Hotel is haunted."

THE HOLLYWOOD CEMETERY THAT'S "FOREVER"

The Hollywood Forever Cemetery has been around for more than 100 years. It contains the graves of 80,000 people, including old-time celebrities such as Rudolph Valentino, Tyrone Power, and Cecil B. Demille. And it features an incredible array of ghostly phenomenon!

PARANORMAL POP QUIZ!

Haunted graveyards are rare, because spirits generally did not have a connection to burial places during their lives, so therefore do not have a reason to return to them. True or false?

(answer: true)

The Crypt of Valentino

Think of the biggest box office star you can imagine. Now double that person's fame in your mind. That's the star power of silent-film actor

Rudolph Valentino in the 1920s! Valentino was a huge star, and although he has been dead for decades, he may still have a faithful fan — a specter who has been spotted at his crypt for years!

Called the "Great Lover" because of his incredible good looks and dashing demeanor, screen legend Valentino's life was cut short in 1926 when he suffered a burst appendix at the age of thirty-one. More than 5,000 mourners attended his funeral, including a mysterious lady dressed in black. And she has visited his grave, mourning, day after day for *years*.

In fact, more than seventy-five years later, many report seeing the ghostly "Lady in Black" lurking near Valentino's crypt. Although her identity remains a mystery, her sad, solitary spirit may be felt at Hollywood Forever Cemetery . . . for eternity.

PHANTOMS OF THE MOVIE STUDIO

From screen legends Charlie Chaplin, Bette Davis, and Joan Crawford to many contemporary stars, Raleigh Studios has been the workplace for Hollywood's greats since it opened in 1915. It's still a popular production site. Many say you can still see people who made moving pictures there long ago, and they haven't aged a bit!

THE PHANTOM FILES

Some people believe that ghosts are actually the remains of repeated activity. The theory says that when an activity occurs over and over in the same place, it may appear like a never-ending video later in that spot. This might explain why the "Lady in Black" returns to Valentino's grave again and again!

Spooky Stage Five

Back in the 1930s, a lone electrician climbed onto a catwalk thirty-five feet above the floor at Stage Five at Raleigh Studios. Nobody is sure what happened next, but the stagehand fell to his death. Ever since, Stage Five has been haunted to the rafters.

One night, when stage managers were closing

Stage Five for the evening, they heard a voice coming from above. Nobody was up on the catwalk. But a huge, 300-pound work light was swinging like crazy! Spooked, the stage managers quickly backed out, shutting the lights and locking the door. Out of curiosity, they returned a few minutes later. They unlocked the door — and found all the lights on again!

THE PHANTOM FILES

Raleigh Studios isn't the only production center that has haunts. Employees at England's Teddington Studios have reported ghostly whispering, falling lighting fixtures, power surges, cold spots, and other supernatural phenomena!

When entering the stage, some people report feeling off-balance. This sensation is followed by an unexplained feeling of tremendous pain in the back and legs.

Odd Occurrences

The strange events at Stage Five are just the start of the supernatural goings-on at Raleigh Studios. Many say a ghostly woman dressed in very old-fashioned clothes is a "regular" in the Studio's Mexican Cantina! Some say she is the spirit of an actress in costume, passing through the cantina on her way to the soundstage to work — still on the job after death!

Once dressing rooms, the studio's office building is also now the site of unexplained paranormal phenomena. An employee reported she felt something grab her from behind when she was working late one night. When she turned around, nothing was there!

Whoever — or *whatever* — grabbed the employee that night remains a mystery. But some say they have seen a strange spirit, dressed as a stagehand. The man lingers at the end of the hallway and stares, vanishing when approached! Other sighting reports include a woman who wears a dress from the 1930s — and walks through walls.

If you could meet any celebrity, who would it be? And if you could encounter

PARANORMAL POP QUIZ!

Renovations in old buildings are said to "stir up" specters. During and after a renovation, many say that ghost sightings increase. True or false?

(answer: true)

the ghost of a late, great movie star, who would you like to see?

The history of Hollywood is filled with legendary stars and forgotten actors, with celebrities who lit up the big screen and those who worked behind the scenes. In the land where legends are made and movie stars lived, both the famous and not-so-famous still show off in death . . . and may live on forever, in haunted Hollywood.

THE PHANTOM FILES

Hollywood's "let's do lunch" takes on a *haunted* new meaning at the Georgian Hotel in nearby Santa Monica! In the hotel dining room, employees report seeing spirits who appear to be old-time movie executives having a meal and talking business. Maybe they're meeting about major motion picture deals!

AMERICA'S MOST HAUNTED: THE ULTIMATE CHALLENGE

Heads up, ghost lovers! Now that you've taken a tour of America's haunted spots, why not test your knowledge of the most ghostly places and faces across the country? (No peeking at the chapters!)

1. **Hollywood Forever is the name of a**
   a. haunted theme restaurant
   b. haunted theme park
   c. haunted cemetery

2. **At the time of the Salem witch trials, an old law stated that a person accused of witchcraft could**
   a. go free if he or she agreed to move to Canada
   b. be crushed until he or she confessed
   c. be entitled to his or her broomstick while in prison

3. **Tombstone, Arizona, was established on land belonging to this group:**
   a. Apache
   b. Iroquois
   c. Choctaw

4. Which famous author is now linked to ghostly activity in Massachusetts?

    a. Nathaniel Hawthorne

    b. Edgar Allan Poe

    c. Jack London

5. The spirit of voodoo queen Marie Laveau is said to sometimes take the form of this animal:

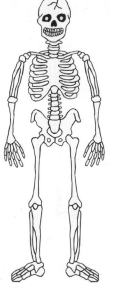

    a. cat

    b. alligator

    c. crow

6. This place was the scene of one of the most famous shootouts in the history of the Wild West:

    a. The K.O. Corral

    b. The O.K. Corral

    c. The Okeydoke Corral

7. In Manitou Springs, Colorado, Emma Crawford sought a cure for

    a. smallpox

    b. fainting spells

    c. tuberculosis

8. **At the Myrtles Plantation, Chloe boiled the leaves of this plant to make a potent poison:**
    a. oleander
    b. magnolia
    c. sweet pea

9. **Marilyn Monroe earned her first money in Hollywood at the Roosevelt Hotel by working as**
    a. a chambermaid
    b. a model
    c. a receptionist

10. **F.O. Stanley owned Colorado's Stanley Hotel, but he was first famous for working with his brother and inventing**
    a. early power tools
    b. a new kind of steam engine
    c. the paper clip

ANSWERS TO AMERICA'S MOST HAUNTED: THE ULTIMATE CHALLENGE

1. c	2. b
3. a	4. a
5. c	6. b
7. c	8. a
9. b	10. b

Scorecard:

If you answered **more than 7** questions correctly, you might want to consider a career as a professional ghost-hunter. Kudos to you for being such a careful reader . . . and such a fearless phantom finder!

If you answered **more than 5** questions correctly, you need to brush up on your spook-seeking skills, but you've still got a good head for ghouls.

If you answered **4 or fewer** questions correctly, you may need to visit some haunted locales yourself to bone up on your ghost-hunting talents . . .

GHOSTLY GLOSSARY

Apparition (a-puh-RIH-shun): the appearance or vision of a person or scene; a ghost.

Clairvoyance (klair-VOY-ants): the ability to gather information paranormally. A *clairvoyant* is a person who may be able to sense and explain ghost activity.

Creole (KREE-ole): originally referred to people of mixed French, Spanish, and sometimes African background who emigrated to Louisiana from the West Indies or Latin America. The term can also refer to the language spoken in parts of Louisiana, which is a dialect of French.

Crypt (KRIHPT): a grave site that may be either above ground or buried underground.

Paranormal (pa-ruh-NOR-muhl): beyond the normal; something that cannot be explained scientifically or through ordinary knowledge.

Parapsychology (PEAR-uh-sye-kahl-uh-gee): the study of paranormal phenomena and/or events. A *parapsychologist* is a person who studies the paranormal.

Phantasm (FAN-ta-zuhm): a ghost or apparition.

Poltergeist (POHL-ter-gyst): a noisy or troublesome spirit. A poltergeist might be responsible for unexplained movement of objects, noises, and physically bothering a person.

Sighting (SYE-teeng): the experience of seeing a ghost.

Specter (SPEHK-ter): a ghost or apparition.

Spiritualism (SPIHR-ih-chuh-wuh-lih-zuhm), *spiritism*: the study and belief in communication between the spirits of the dead and the living.

LEARN ALL ABOUT THE WORLD'S WEIRDEST CREATURES!
READ

THE HISTORY CHANNEL® PRESENTS
HISTORY'S MYSTERIES®: BIZARRE BEINGS

What are mummies made of? Are alien bodies hidden somewhere on Earth? What does the Loch Ness monster eat for breakfast? You'll find answers to these questions — and much, much more — in this chronicle of the world's creepiest creatures. You'll dive under the ocean to come face-to-face with some seriously scary water monsters and you'll travel back in time to see what cavemen looked like.

Packed with quizzes, real-life photos, and zillions of weird facts, *Bizarre Beings* just might make you believe . . . in the unbelievable!